A Prehistoric Puzzle

"Students, I have some bad news," said Ms. Vaughn, the principal. "Mr. Clark's presentation for today has been canceled. The reason is that the iguanodon model is missing."

Everyone groaned.

"And," Ms. Vaughn said, "if the model isn't found by the end of the week, we will have to cancel the entire event."

"This is the pits!" Tanya Wilkins said.

"I can't believe it," Chet Morton said.

"What are we going to do?" Tony Prito asked.

"There's only one thing to do," Frank said.

"I know what that is," Joe said. "We're going to have to crack this case—before the exhibit becomes extinct."

Frank and Joe Hardy: The Clues Brothers

#1 The Gross Ghost Mystery
#2 The Karate Clue
#3 First Day, Worst Day
#4 Jump Shot Detectives
#5 Dinosaur Disaster

Available from MINSTREL BOOKS

FRANK AND JOE HARDY: THE CLUES BROTHERS™

DINOSAUR DISASTER

Franklin W. Dixon

Illustrated by
Marcy Ramsey

A MINSTREL® BOOK

Published by POCKET BOOKS
New York London Toronto Sydney Tokyo Singapore

A MINSTREL PAPERBACK *Original*

 A Minstrel Book published by
POCKET BOOKS, a division of Simon & Schuster Inc.
1230 Avenue of the Americas, New York, NY 10020

Copyright © 1998 by Simon & Schuster Inc.

Front cover illustration by Thompson Studio

Produced by Mega-Books, Inc.

ISBN: 0-671-00406-9

First Minstrel Books printing March 1998

10 9 8 7 6 5 4 3 2 1

1

Lights, Camera . . . Action!

Third-grader Joe Hardy dropped his backpack and began to run across the blacktop behind Bayport Elementary School. "That car looks awesome! Let's check it out," he shouted to his nine-year-old brother, Frank.

At the other end of the parking lot, sixth-grader Carlos Mendez was playing with a remote-control car.

"Cool car," Joe said. He turned his baseball cap backward. "Can I try it out?"

"Sure," Carlos said. He handed the controls to Joe. "Be careful, though. Mike will be very angry if you mess up anything."

Mike was Carlos's younger brother and a friend of Frank and Joe's.

Joe steered the car in a few big circles. Then he gave Frank a turn.

"How come Mike wasn't in school today?" Joe asked Carlos.

"He's home with a cold," Carlos said. Then he turned to Frank. "Hey, watch out for that van," he said.

The three boys stood back as a large van pulled into the parking lot. Two men hopped down from the high front seat of the van. They opened a side door. Then they began unloading a movie projector, a screen, and several large boxes.

"Wow!" Joe said. "That must be the stuff for tomorrow's assembly."

"I can't believe it. Mark Clark is going to be right here at our school," Frank said.

"Yeah, and he's going to tell us all his secrets about his dinosaur movies," Carlos added.

Mark Clark was a film director who made movies with very realistic-looking dinosaurs.

The boys watched as the two men carried a heavy-looking crate across the blacktop and through the side door of the school. The side door led directly to the auditorium.

"I'll bet that's the iguanodon," Frank said.

"Mike *has* to be here to see how it works," Joe told Carlos. "Let's look in through the windows and watch them unpack it."

"The shades are down," Carlos said. "We won't be able to see anything inside. I guess we'll have to wait until tomorrow."

"Tomorrow we'll see it live and in living color. Just like on my backpack," Joe said.

He picked up the backpack he'd dropped. He showed Carlos the scene on it. The scene was from Mark Clark's new movie, *Night of the Iguanodon*. The dinosaur was snarling and ripping up a tree by its roots.

Just then a car pulled into the parking lot. A man and a woman got out and walked toward the auditorium.

"Hello, boys," the man said as they approached Joe, Frank, and Carlos. "I'm Mark Clark. And this is Dr. Carol Gershwin. She's a paleontologist."

"You look at fossils, right?" Joe asked Dr. Gershwin eagerly. Joe read everything he could about dinosaurs.

"Yes," Dr. Gershwin said. "I study dinosaur bones to find out how long ago each type of dinosaur lived. I'll tell you a lot more tomorrow."

"Dr. Gershwin helps me on all my films," Mark Clark said. "That's why the dinosaurs are so realistic. Tomorrow we'll autograph our new book for you.

It's called *Making Movie Magic*. We'll show you some movie clips. And then everyone will get to check out some of the actual movie models up close."

"One of them is going to be the iguanodon model, right?" Joe said.

"That's right," Mr. Clark said with a chuckle. "I'm happy that you know so much about our work."

Mr. Clark looked at Carlos's car. "That looks like a powerful remote you've got," he said.

"It sure is. My brother, Mike, fixed it up so it's extra powerful," Carlos said. "He can't wait to check out the iguanodon's wiring system."

"He's going to love it. We used special technology to make the model look more lifelike when it moves on the screen," Dr. Gershwin said.

Then Dr. Gershwin lowered her voice, as if she were telling a secret. "And you know, other special-effects artists would love to know how Mark does it. It would

6

be worth a lot of money to them to get hold of the model."

"Wow!" Joe said. He knew the model must be valuable, but he never would have guessed other people would want to steal its secrets.

"Can we have a sneak peek at the iguanodon, Mr. Clark?" Carlos asked.

"I'd love to show it to you. But it will take us a while to set everything up," Mr. Clark said. "I'm sure you'll all be home having dinner by then."

"We'll see you tomorrow," Dr. Gershwin said.

Each of the boys thanked Dr. Gershwin and Mr. Clark for taking the time to talk with them. Then Frank and Joe said goodbye to Carlos. They got on their bikes and headed home.

On Tuesday morning, when Frank and Joe arrived at school, everyone was chattering with excitement.

"I'm all set. I've got on my iguanodon

hat and my iguanodon T-shirt today," Tanya Wilkins said. Tanya was in fourth grade.

Kevin Saris, a third-grader, said, "I've seen all of Mark Clark's movies. This is going to be great!"

When the classes had lined up outside to go into their rooms, the principal spoke to them through her megaphone.

"Students," Ms. Vaughn said, holding one hand up for silence. "I'm afraid I have some bad news. Mr. Clark's presentation for today has been canceled."

Everyone groaned. Then Ms. Vaughn said, "The reason is that the iguanodon model is missing."

Now everyone started talking at once.

Ms. Vaughn waited a moment and then continued. "Dr. Gershwin and Mr. Clark have agreed to sell and autograph books today as planned. But since the model was the main part of the presentation, those events will be postponed until the model has been found.

"And," Ms. Vaughn said, "if the model isn't found by the end of the week, we will have to cancel the entire event."

"This is the pits!" Tanya said.

"I can't believe it," Chet Morton said. Chet was one of Frank and Joe's best friends. He was also in Frank's fourth-grade class.

"What are we going to do?" Tony Prito asked. Tony was a classmate of Joe's.

"There's only one thing to do," Frank said.

"I know what that is," Joe said. "We're going to have to crack this case—before the exhibit becomes extinct."

2

Plots, Plans, and Pals

Frank sat down at his desk in Mrs. Burton's classroom. He wanted to think of ways to begin solving the case. Mrs. Burton called for the class's attention so she could start their spelling lesson. Frank knew he would have to wait.

When Frank had finished making up sentences using the new words Mrs. Burton had written on the board, he passed a note to Chet. The note said: "We have to make a list." At the bottom Frank had spelled out the word *suspects*.

Chet nodded. He wrote back: "We can talk at recess."

As soon as the bell rang, Frank and Chet ran for the door. They found Joe on the playground. He was with a group of boys who were picking teams for a basketball game.

When the game began, Frank was on the same team as Chet. They were playing with Tony Prito and a third-grader named Malcolm. On the other team was Kevin Saris, a boy named Biff Hooper, Joe, and Malcolm's younger cousin, whose name was Brad.

"We need to make our list of suspects," Frank said. He ran down the court and blocked one of Kevin's shots. Then he passed the ball to Tony.

"But we don't have any clues," Joe said.

Tony dribbled the ball around Joe. "Who else was there yesterday when you guys met Dr. Gershwin and Mr. Clark?" he asked. Tony took a shot and made it.

As the boys ran to the other end of the court, Joe said, "Carlos was playing with Mike's remote-control car. He said Mike could hardly wait to see the iguanodon's wiring system. I guess that means Mike could be a suspect."

"But Mike wasn't there," Frank said. He brushed his brown hair out of his eyes. "I can't believe Mike would take anything."

Chet had the ball, and he threw it to Frank. "Did you see anything suspicious yesterday afternoon?" he asked.

Frank didn't answer right away. He was running under the basket for a layup. But Biff jumped in, stole the ball from him, and scored. Then the bell rang.

"Now the game's tied," Joe said.

"We can finish it after lunch," Kevin said.

As they walked back to their classrooms, Frank thought about Tony's question.

12

"I don't know if I saw anything suspicious," he said. "We saw two men wheel some boxes into the auditorium. The boxes were about the size of televisions."

"They probably held the smaller models for the hands-on exhibit," Tony said.

"Probably," Joe said. "Then we saw a bigger crate being unloaded. We guessed that was the iguanodon."

"That means the model must be big—and hard to carry," Tony said.

"You got it," Frank said. "I'd say the model must be the same size as your dog Boof." He spread his arms to show the size and height of the box.

At lunch Joe, Frank, Chet, and Tanya discussed the case.

"It's not fair that Mr. Clark and Dr. Gershwin's talk was postponed," Chet said. He opened his container of milk and stuck a straw into it.

"I'll help solve the mystery," Tanya said. She took some potato chips from her bag and began crunching loudly.

"Fine with us," Frank said. "We can use all the help we can get."

"Today's Tuesday. We have three days before Ms. Vaughn cancels everything," Tanya said. "Counting today, we have three and a half days."

A boy named Brett moved closer to the group. "You're not going to get any help from me," he said.

"Good," Tanya said. "Because no one asked you to help." Brett was a member of a group of bullies known as the Zack Pack. They were named after their leader, Zack Jackson.

Brett ignored Tanya's comment. "I have my own model dinosaur collection at home. It's bigger and better than anything you would've seen at the assembly, anyway."

"I'll bet it isn't," Joe said. He peeled a banana and added half of it to his peanut butter sandwich.

"It is, too," Brett said. "I even have a special new model."

"Big deal," Chet said. He squashed his empty milk carton. Then he tossed it into the garbage pail as if he were shooting a basket.

"If you guys don't believe me, you can come over to my house and see for yourselves," Brett said. His face was turning as red as his fruit punch.

"Maybe we'll do that," Frank said.

"Go ahead and come over," Brett said. "For fifty cents, I'll prove it to you."

"Fifty cents?" Chet slammed his lunch box shut. "Are you kidding? I personally wouldn't go to your house for more than twenty-five cents."

"It's a deal," Brett said quickly. "See you all later. Be at my house at three o'clock sharp. And don't be late."

As Brett was walking away from the table, Frank said, "Who does he think he is? Charging admission to his room."

"It's worth it to me," Joe said. "I really want to see his model collection. Count me in."

16

"What do you think, guys?" Tanya asked. "Do you think the special new addition to his collection will look like an iguanodon?"

"Maybe," Chet said.

"Even if his model is an iguanodon, we don't have any proof that he took it," Frank said.

"We might," Tanya said. "Yesterday, after school, my mom came late to pick me up. When we drove away, I saw Brett go back into the school building. He walked around to the side entrance— where the auditorium is. I think he's the one who took it."

"We might find out when we go to his house," Frank said. "My guess is that Mark Clark's iguanodon is bigger than the models that Brett has. So when we get there, we'll just look all around his room for it."

"I wish we could look when he's not in the room," Joe said. "Then we could look in his closet or under the bed."

Chet smiled. "I'll be in charge of getting him out of his room. Then we can look around."

When the bell rang, they all got up from the tables to stack their trays and throw the garbage away.

"Come on, let's finish our game," Kevin Saris called. Even though Kevin hadn't made the school team, he enjoyed playing basketball.

As the group left the cafeteria, Frank whispered to Joe, "I've been thinking that Carlos should be a suspect, too. He was there."

"No way," Joe said. "Carlos didn't take the model, and neither did Mike."

"Remember how Carlos told Dr. Gershwin about Mike wanting to see the model's wiring system so badly? Carlos could have taken the model *for* Mike," Frank said.

"Mike is one of our best friends, and Carlos is his brother. He can't be guilty," Joe said.

"You know what Dad always says," Frank replied. " 'Look at the facts.' Well, the facts show that Carlos was there around the time that the iguanodon might have been taken. You have to admit that he could have taken it."

"Oh, okay," Joe said.

As Joe walked to Mrs. Adair's class, he thought about the case. He wasn't sure which he felt sadder about—the missing dinosaur model or having to add Carlos to the list of suspects.

Now we really have to solve the mystery—and fast, Joe thought.

3

Stop, Thief!

As soon as school let out, Frank and Joe called their mother to get permission to go over to Brett's. Mrs. Hardy said yes and told them to be home in two hours.

When Frank and Joe got to the bike racks, Tanya and Chet were waiting for them.

"Where's Brett?" Frank asked.

"His mom picked him up," Chet said. "He said he'll meet us at his house."

"At three o'clock sharp," Tanya,

Frank, and Joe said at the same time. Then they all laughed.

The friends got on their bikes and rode down the shady Bayport streets to Brett's house. When they rang the bell, Brett opened the front door. "Twenty-five cents, please," he said as he stretched out his hand.

"This better be good," Chet said. He handed Brett five nickels. Frank dug into his pocket and found a quarter. Joe put a nickel and two dimes into Brett's hand.

Tanya had only a dollar bill, so Brett gave her the seventy-five cents that the others had given him.

Once everyone had paid to see the dinosaur models, Brett led them upstairs.

"Wow!" Joe shouted as they entered Brett's bedroom. "I don't believe it!"

"Told you so," Brett said. He crossed his arms over his chest and grinned.

Brett's room had the best collection of toy dinosaur models any of them had ever seen. There were models on Brett's

shelves, on his desk, around his desk, over his bed, and even on the window sills.

"You have more models than I have Jimmy Han posters," Tanya said. Tanya was a big fan of the karate star Jimmy Han. She was also president of his fan club.

"Mark Clark should make a movie with Jimmy Han," Joe said.

"Karate and dinosaurs," Brett said. "That's a good combination."

"Yeah, the best!" Chet said.

"Look at this megalosaurus," Tanya said. She picked up a model the size of a basketball.

Joe touched the megalosaurus model. "Just think, a real one of these monsters would have weighed one ton," he said.

Chet bent down to study the larger models on the floor beside Brett's desk. One of them had thick plastic armor plates running down its back. "What's this one?" Chet asked.

"It's a stegosaurus," Brett said proudly.

"That looks so real," Joe said. "Do you ever get scared at night sleeping in here with all these dinosaurs?" he asked.

"Not me," Brett said. He sat down in the desk chair and put his feet up on the desk. "Nothing scares me," he said. He jabbed his chest with his thumb.

Joe touched the wide head and the stumpy legs of another model. He ran his hand down the long, thick tail.

"I have *two* of those allosaurus models," Brett said.

"No way! I've seen these at Hooper's Hobby Shop. They cost a fortune," Joe said.

"I do so have two," Brett said. "But my dad had to take the other one back to Hooper's to be repaired. They're battery-operated, and the wires were crossed. It wasn't working right."

"That's cool," Tanya said. "You can make them move all around your room?"

"Just like in one of Mark Clark's movies," Joe said.

Frank was glad the others were talking to Brett. It gave him a chance to look around the room for the iguanodon. He didn't see it out anywhere.

Then Frank noticed a book sticking out of Brett's backpack. He pulled it out just far enough so he could see the title.

"Don't look at that!" Brett cried out. He jumped up from his chair and tried to kick the book back into his backpack.

Frank was too quick for him. He reached down and picked up the book. "Hey, this is all about the iguanodon," Frank said.

Brett tried to grab the book out of Frank's hands.

"Why do you have a whole book about iguanodons?" Frank asked.

"And why were you sneaking back into school yesterday?" Tanya asked.

"Yeah, and why haven't you shown us

25

your new model if it's so great?" Joe asked.

Brett was surrounded. He looked at each of the faces that had gathered around him. But he didn't say anything.

"Did you take the model, Brett?" Tanya asked. "Is that the special new addition you were bragging about?"

"No!" Brett said. "Just because I have a book about iguanodons doesn't mean I took the model."

"It's pretty strong evidence," Tanya said.

"Besides," Brett said, "you were at school late yesterday, too. Maybe *you* took the model."

"I did not!" Tanya shouted. She planted her hands on her hips. "I was there waiting for my mom to pick me up. I was outside the school. You were the one who went inside."

"Well, I can explain," Brett said. "I was there because, because . . . " he said, but then he stopped.

Brett and Tanya glared at each other.

"Come on, you two. Quit fighting," Joe said.

"If you didn't take it, who did, Brett?" Frank asked. "Why don't you finish explaining?"

But before Brett had a chance to explain anything, Chet looked out the window.

"Oh, no!" he yelled. "All our bikes have been stolen from the yard!"

4

Caught in the Act

All the kids bumped into one another as they tried to get out of Brett's room.

"Time out!" Frank shouted. He made a "T" sign with his hands. "Our bikes aren't out there." He walked over to the window.

"See?" he said. "Brett's room faces the backyard. We left our bikes in the front."

Everyone stared at Chet.

Chet stared at the floor. Then he said, "I was just trying to get Brett out of the room so we could look around, remember?"

Brett shook his head. "First you guys accuse me of a crime I didn't commit, and then you plan to search my room!"

"Well, you have to admit you've been acting kind of funny," Chet said.

"I didn't take the iguanodon model. I'll prove that it's not here," Brett said. He began tearing his room apart. He opened all his drawers. He pushed back his curtains. He even dumped his laundry basket out onto the floor.

"Phew," Chet said, holding his nose. "Okay, okay, I believe you."

"*I* don't believe you," Tanya said.

So Brett turned around and lifted the blanket on his bed so they could look underneath it. Then he flung open the closet door.

"See?" he said.

"Showing us that it's not in your room doesn't prove you don't have it," Frank said. "You could have it hidden someplace else."

"Yeah, maybe we should search the whole house," Joe said.

"Or maybe it's with your other allosaurus," Tanya said.

"It's not," Brett said. Suddenly Brett looked sad instead of angry. He went back to his desk and sat down in his chair. Then he put his head in his hands.

"Listen, I really do have another allosaurus that's being fixed. But I haven't shown you my special new model because I don't have that one yet," he said. "I just said that because I wanted you guys to *think* I had it."

"You might as well tell us what happened, Brett. We're going to find out anyway," Frank said.

"All right, here goes," Brett said with a sigh. "Mr. Sterling, the custodian, let me into the side entrance of the building late yesterday afternoon. It was because the front doors of the school were locked.

"The reason I had to go back in was that I left the dinosaur book in my locker.

I was reading about the iguanodon because it's the only dinosaur I don't have in my collection. I found a great picture, and I wanted to show it to my parents. That way they'd know which model to get me for my birthday next week."

"I guess that explains things," Chet said after Brett had finished.

"Yeah, I believe you," Frank said.

"I think you might be off the suspect list," Joe said.

"For now," Tanya added.

"Good," Brett said. He walked over to his allosaurus and flipped the on button. The dinosaur began to walk across the carpet.

"Help, I'm being attacked!" Chet said as it walked over his sneaker.

"I'll protect you," Tanya said, doing a pretend karate kick. She was careful not to knock over the dinosaur.

"Karate and dinosaurs are the best," Joe said.

The group played with Brett's dinosaurs until Frank noticed the time on his watch. "It's four-thirty. We'd better get going," he said to Joe.

When everyone went downstairs, Brett's mother said, "Honey, did you show your friends the picture of the model you want for your birthday?"

"I sure did, Mom," Brett said.

At the door Tanya paused for a second. Then she said, "I hope you get that model for your birthday. You've got a great collection."

"Thanks," Brett said with a grin. "See you later."

The friends got on their bikes and headed for their homes.

"You know, Brett's not so bad when he's not with the rest of the Zack Pack," Tanya said.

"That's true," Joe said. "But what are we going to do now for a suspect?"

"Keep digging for clues, I guess," Frank said.

"But we don't have any more leads," Chet said.

"Our dad always tells us that a good detective never gives up until the mystery is solved," Frank said.

Frank and Joe's father, Fenton Hardy, had been a detective in New York before they moved to Bayport. He often helped the boys with their cases.

Joe and Chet pedaled behind Frank and Tanya. Their route home took them past Bayport Elementary. When they got to the parking lot of the school, Tanya stopped and said, "Look! It's Dr. Gershwin."

Tanya pointed to the side door of the school, right where the auditorium was.

The others stopped, too, and hopped off their bikes. Dr. Gershwin was kneeling on the ground beside the auditorium door. She was covering a very large object with a blanket. Then she picked up the object and began to walk across the parking lot.

"What do you think she's carrying?" Joe said.

"I don't know," Frank said. "But it sure looks heavy. Kind of like the iguanodon."

Dr. Gershwin was heading for the only car left in the parking lot.

"Do you think it could be the model?" Tanya said.

"It has to be," Chet said.

They steered their bikes into the parking lot. Dr. Gershwin balanced the object on the trunk of her car and took out her car keys.

"Maybe Dr. Gershwin is a spy working for those other special-effects people," Frank said. "Remember she told us how valuable the model was?"

"And they're going to give her lots of money for Mr. Clark's secret technique that makes the model move so smoothly," Joe said.

"I'll bet you're right," Frank said. "I think we've caught our dinosaur thief—red-handed!"

5

False Alarm

The bicycle riders rode into the parking lot and skidded to a stop in front of Dr. Gershwin.

"Well, hello," Dr. Gershwin said. She smiled at Frank and Joe. "You're the Hardy brothers, right? I remember you from yesterday. Who are your friends?"

"This is Tanya," Frank said, jumping off his bike.

"And Chet," Joe said. He jumped off his bike, too. "That looks heavy, Dr.

Gershwin. Can we help you get the dino—I mean, that thing into the car?

"Oh, you mean my computer printer?" Dr. Gershwin said. She pulled the blanket back to show the printer. "Yes, that would be nice. Can you open the trunk for me?"

Dr. Gershwin held the printer while Frank and Joe lifted the trunk lid of the car. Then Dr. Gershwin carefully placed the printer inside. "It's so dusty in here," she said. "I had to find something to wrap this printer in."

Dr. Gershwin slammed the trunk shut. "Now, what did you think my printer was?"

"We kind of thought it might be the missing iguanodon," Frank said.

"And why would I be putting the iguanodon model wrapped in a blanket into the trunk of my car?" Dr. Gershwin asked. She had a puzzled look on her face.

Joe didn't want her to know they had

thought she was a spy. "Maybe it had a dino-*sore*, and you were taking it to the doctor!"

Joe was happy when everyone laughed at his joke, including Dr. Gershwin.

When they stopped giggling, Tanya said, "Actually, Frank and Joe solve mysteries. We call them the Clues Brothers."

"That's right," Chet said. "And with our help, they're going to find the missing iguanodon model."

Dr. Gershwin sighed. "I hope you do. I enjoy the shows that Mark and I give. And students about your age make up the most enthusiastic audiences."

"That's why we're on the case. We've been investigating all day," Chet said.

"Well, I'm going to be working late tonight, too," Dr. Gershwin said as she patted Chet on the shoulder. "I'll be working on the plans to build a new model," she said. "That's why I'm bringing this printer home. I hope to finish tonight and print out the new drawings."

"We promise to keep searching for clues and suspects," Frank said.

"But right now we have to be home for dinner," Joe said.

"Investigating makes me hungry," Chet said.

"*Everything* makes you hungry," Tanya said with a grin.

Frank, Joe, Chet, and Tanya called goodbye to Dr. Gershwin and pedaled to their homes.

At dinner Frank and Joe told their parents about the missing iguanodon. Mr. Hardy stroked his chin, deep in thought, as he listened to the details.

Then he took a sip of coffee and a bite of the deep-dish peach pie Mrs. Hardy had served for dessert.

"It sounds as if you boys are doing a terrific job so far. You're investigating your suspects carefully, and you're following up on all your leads. Just remember, it's important to keep your eyes and

ears open at all times. Question everyone. Don't leave any stone unturned,"
he said.

"Okay, Dad," Frank said.

As Frank and Joe got ready for bed,
they talked about what their father had
said.

"I wonder if we're leaving any stones
unturned," Joe said.

"I don't think so, but let's sleep on it,"
Frank replied.

"I think I'd rather sleep on my soft pil-
low," Joe said.

"Ha, ha," Frank said. Before Joe could
tell any other jokes, both boys were
sound asleep.

On Wednesday morning Frank and Joe
left for school early. They each wanted
to find a new book to read. They headed
for the library as soon as they reached
school.

Joe was flipping through a book about
baseball when he saw Carlos sitting at a

table in the corner of the library. Joe could see that Carlos was reading a copy of the new edition of the school newspaper.

Joe tiptoed over to Frank, who was reading a book about the Civil War.

"Hey, Frank," Joe said. "Last night Dad said we should question everyone. Do you think we should ask Carlos if he took the model for Mike?"

"Yeah, we can't leave any stones unturned," Frank said. They walked over to the table where Carlos was sitting.

"Hi, Carlos," Frank said.

"Mind if we sit down?" Joe asked.

"I don't usually let third- and fourth-graders sit with me, but since you're friends of my brother, I guess it's okay," Carlos replied with a grin. "What's up?"

Joe decided just to blurt out the question. "Carlos, did you take the model for Mike?"

"No way. I'd never take anything that didn't belong to me!" Carlos said angrily.

"Shh," the librarian, Ms. Goldberg, said. "Quiet, boys."

"Do you think Mike would have taken it?" Joe asked in a whisper.

"Not in a million years," Carlos whispered back. "Besides, he's been home with a cold, remember?"

"But you said he could hardly wait to see the iguanodon's wiring system," Frank said.

"That's true. Mike would give almost anything for a look at that wiring. But that doesn't include stealing. Neither of us would do anything like that," Carlos said.

"Not even as a joke or just to look at it and return it?" Frank asked.

"Not even," Carlos assured them.

Just then Frank noticed the big headline in the school paper that Carlos had been reading. "Look at that!" Frank said.

Joe looked at the paper on the table. Then he read out loud, " 'Principal Says: Make No Bones About It—The Show Will Not Go On.' "

Frank looked the name under the headline. "Kevin Saris wrote this article," he said.

Kevin Saris was a reporter for the school paper.

"Can I read the article?" Joe asked.

"Sure," Carlos said. He handed the paper to Joe.

"It's all about the missing model," Joe said after he had read a few paragraphs. "It's very detailed. I wonder how he knows all these facts."

When Joe had finished the article, he handed the paper to his brother. As Frank read, he stroked his chin the way he had seen his father do.

Frank put the paper down. "You're right, Joe. Something is fishy about this. Kevin couldn't know so much about the model if he never saw it."

"He couldn't know that much about it unless . . ." Joe said. "Unless he's the one who took it!"

6

The Chase Is On

Can we hang on to this paper for evidence?" Joe asked Carlos.

"No problem. Good luck, you guys," Carlos said.

Joe stuffed the paper into his back pocket and thanked Carlos.

"Guess what stone we're going to turn during recess?" Frank asked. "Meet me by the door as soon as Mrs. Adair lets your class out."

Joe was happy that they were learning

about the early settlers in their history class. He loved reading about how people lived hundreds of years ago. It made the morning go quickly. As soon as the bell rang for recess, Joe ran to meet his brother.

Frank and Joe looked everywhere for Kevin. They looked on the playground, in the gym, and back in the classroom. But they didn't see him anywhere, even at lunch.

"Maybe he got sick and went home," Joe said.

"Or maybe he's hiding from us," Frank said. "We'd better keep an eye out for him."

After lunch Chet passed a note to Frank. It said: "I looked for you at lunch. Where were you guys?"

Frank passed the note back to Chet. Underneath Chet's note, Frank had written: "We have another suspect. Meet us after school at the bike rack."

Chet gave Frank a thumbs-up sign,

and the boys went back to their silent reading.

At the end of the day, Frank walked to Joe's classroom.

"Hurry," Joe called. "Kevin was called into Ms. Vaughn's office," he said.

"Why would he be going to her office after school?" Frank asked.

"I don't know," Joe said. "But let's stick to him like glue this time."

"Okay," Frank said. The boys began to walk toward Ms. Vaughn's office. They tried to keep a safe distance from Kevin. When he stopped to tie his sneaker lace, Frank and Joe crouched behind a water fountain.

They stayed that way while Kevin walked down the hall. When he entered Ms. Vaughn's office, Frank and Joe kept their eyes on the office door. Suddenly Frank felt a tap on his shoulder.

"Ahh!" Frank screamed, and jumped into the air.

"Ahh!" Joe yelled. "You scared me!"

"Ahh!" Chet shouted. "You guys are so scared, you scared me!"

"Why did you sneak up on us like that?" Frank asked.

"You told me to meet you after school," Chet said. "I waited at the bike rack, and then I came back in to find you."

"Oh, right," Frank said.

"You look really silly hiding behind this water fountain," Chet said. "You said you had another suspect. Is that why you're spying on the office?"

"Yes," Frank said. "Kevin's in there. We think he might have taken the iguanodon."

"He wrote all about it in the paper. We think the only way he could have known so much is if he's the one who took it," Joe said.

"Plus," Frank said, "he's been avoiding us all day."

"So we're following him," Joe said.

"Hey, there he goes!" Frank said.

The boys saw Kevin rush out of Ms. Vaughn's office. He closed the office door, looked around, then starting walking quickly down the hall toward the exit. Frank, Joe, and Chet followed him.

"Be careful," Frank said. "We don't want him to see us."

Kevin had begun to walk so quickly that he was almost at the end of the hallway. Frank, Joe, and Chet began to run.

"Boys!" A voice thundered down the hallway. Frank, Joe, and Chet turned to see Ms. Vaughn standing in the doorway to her office. Her arms were folded.

"Have you boys forgotten the no-running-in-the-halls rule?" she asked.

"We're sorry, Ms. Vaughn," Frank said.

"We'll slow down," Chet said.

"Thank you," Ms. Vaughn said. She disappeared into her office.

When she had closed her office door, the boys walked as fast as they could without running. When they reached the

exit door Kevin had used, they saw him getting on his bike.

"Hurry," Frank called. The three boys ran for the bike racks, unlocked their bikes, and jumped on. But by then Kevin was rounding the corner and heading up the street.

"Hurry, or we'll lose him again!" Frank shouted over his shoulder.

The boys pedaled quickly. They spotted Kevin just before he turned again.

"He's heading for his parents' pizza parlor," Joe said.

They followed Kevin until they saw him park his bike beside the back door of Pizza Paradise. Then he disappeared inside.

Frank, Joe, and Chet parked their bikes and walked around to the front of the restaurant.

"We'll order a few slices," Chet said.

"Why did I know you were going to say that?" Frank said with a grin.

Joe shook his head. "Don't you ever think of anything besides dinner?"

"Of course," Chet said. "I think about dessert, too!"

Frank and Joe laughed. "We have to call home before we order, so Mom won't worry about us," Frank said. Chet called his mother also, even though he said she never worried about him spoiling his appetite.

At the counter, each boy ordered a slice of pizza and a soda. They could see Kevin in the back, helping his father roll out pizza dough.

"It sure must be hot back there in the kitchen," Frank said.

"It's hot out here. Especially after that fast bike ride," Joe said. He took the copy of the school newspaper out of his back pocket. He began fanning himself with it.

Kevin turned and saw his friends standing at the counter. His eyes opened wide as he stared at Joe.

"I think Kevin thinks Joe is waving that newspaper at him," Frank said.

"Maybe he knows we're onto him," Chet said.

"What if he runs away again?" Joe asked.

"I don't think he's running anymore," Frank said.

Slowly, Kevin walked out of the kitchen. He came over to the boys. He wiped his flour-covered hands on his apron.

"I guess you guys read my article," Kevin said.

"We sure did," Joe said.

"And you didn't come over here just to get some pizza, did you?" Kevin asked.

"Nope," Frank said.

"We were wondering how come you know so much about the iguanodon," Joe began.

"If you never saw it," Chet finished.

Kevin looked down at the floor. "Okay, okay," he said. "I'll tell you everything that happened."

7

Kevin Makes a Confession

The thing is," Kevin began, "I actually got to see the iguanodon before it was stolen."

"How do we know *you* didn't steal the iguanodon?" Chet said.

"Me? Steal the iguanodon? No way!" Kevin said. "I just felt terrible because I didn't tell you guys I got to meet Mark Clark and see the model before the show."

"Why didn't you tell us?" Frank asked.

"In case the model wasn't found, I didn't want you to be mad at me for seeing it," Kevin said.

"How come you got to see it?" Joe asked.

"Let's go sit down, and I'll explain everything," Kevin said.

The boys picked up their sodas and their steaming slices of cheese pizza. Kevin led them to a booth, and they slid into their seats.

"I stayed really late after school on Monday. I was working on my article about the special assembly," Kevin said.

"I was passing the auditorium on the way out. That's when I saw Mr. Clark unpacking the iguanodon. I asked him if I could see it and interview him."

"What happened next?" Joe asked. He was making notes on a pad he had taken from his iguanodon backpack.

Kevin told the boys all about his meeting with Mr. Clark. "The interview was

great. It's everything else that's a mess," he said with a sigh.

"What do you mean?" Frank asked.

"My next article is going to be about making recess longer. I had asked Ms. Vaughn if I could interview her. And before I left school today, I went to her office."

"A longer recess? Cool!" Chet said.

"Yeah, what's so bad about that?" Joe asked.

"The bad part is what I heard Ms. Vaughn say. She was busy when I got there. So I waited," Kevin said. He wiped some tomato sauce from his mouth with a corner of his apron and went on.

"That's when I overheard her on the phone. She was saying that if the model wasn't found by tomorrow, Mr. Clark and Dr. Gershwin were going to pack up everything, and she was going to cancel the show!"

All Joe had left on his plate was his

pizza crust. He held it up to his face to make a pizza crust frown. "But we haven't found the iguanodon yet," he said sadly.

"And we've run out of suspects," Frank said.

"We're out of clues, too. And I'm out of soda," Chet said. He slurped the last of his drink.

"We'll talk to our dad. He'll help us figure out what to do next," Frank said.

The Hardy boys said goodbye and went around back to get their bikes. On their way home, they passed Bayport Elementary School. On the blacktop near the auditorium, they saw Carlos playing with Mike's remote-control car.

"Hi, Carlos," Frank said, getting off his bike.

"Hi. You guys solve the mystery yet?" Carlos asked.

"No," Joe said, parking his bike. "Kevin was innocent."

"What did he say?" Carlos asked.

"Nothing that would help," Joe said as he took out his notepad. He tore out a sheet of paper and scrunched it into a tight ball.

"Anything could help," Carlos said. "You never know where you might find clues."

"Carlos is right," Frank said. "Let's try to figure this thing out one last time—before it's too late."

"Okay," Joe said. He unfolded the crumpled paper and looked at his notes again. "Kevin told us that when he got to the auditorium, Mr. Clark was just taking the iguanodon out of its crate. He let Kevin look at it."

"So," Carlos said, "that's why he knew so much about it."

"Yes," Frank said. "Kevin said that after he looked at the iguanodon, Mr. Clark put it on the floor under one of the tables. He covered it with some plastic. Then Kevin asked him lots of questions about the model."

"Kevin said he and Mr. Clark left together. Mr. Sterling locked the door behind them," Joe said.

"Mr. Sterling could have taken the model," Carlos said.

"Mr. Sterling? Why do you think so?" Frank asked Carlos.

"Because on Monday, the day the model was stolen, Mr. Sterling came outside and told me I should stop playing with my car. He said he had a lot of work to do fixing some electrical problems in the building and that I should go home. I left pretty much right after you guys did."

"That doesn't make Mr. Sterling a suspect," Joe said.

"But maybe he said those things to me because he didn't want any witnesses around when he took the model out of the auditorium," Carlos said.

"I don't know," Frank said. "Mr. Sterling's a really nice guy."

"Yeah, and he seems to like us kids a lot," Joe added.

"You're right," Carlos said after a moment. "You know," he added, "even detectives need to take their minds off their cases for a little while. Do you guys want to see how Mike rigged up this car?"

"Sure," Frank said. "That would be neat."

Carlos picked up the car and turned it over. "Mike added some wires so that the remote control would be more powerful," he said.

Joe looked at the underside of the car. He noticed several extra wires. Some of them had been twisted together. Joe could see that Mike had added two extra batteries. "No wonder the signal is so strong," he said. "Mike added more juice."

"I'll bet the remote control could work from much farther than with other cars," Frank said.

Carlos let Frank and Joe each have another turn with the car. Frank was steering the car in a large figure eight all the way across the parking lot when the boys heard a loud crash coming from inside the auditorium.

"That could be the thief!" Frank shouted.

"Could he have come back to take another one of the models before the exhibit leaves?" Joe asked.

"I don't know," Frank said. "But we're about to find out."

8

Dinosaur Detectives

The boys ran to a side window of the auditorium. The shade on one window had been raised a little bit. The boys stood on tiptoe and peered in through the darkened window.

"Look at all those models on the floor," Frank said.

"Maybe the thief knocked them over," Joe said. "We've got to get inside and catch him before he gets away again."

The boys banged on the auditorium

door. After about a minute, Mr. Sterling opened it. "Where's the fire, boys? The alarm didn't go off."

"There's no fire," Joe said. "But we think the thief who stole the iguanodon is in the auditorium right now."

"Calm down," Mr. Sterling said. "There's no thief in this building. I've just locked everything up, and I didn't see anyone."

"Mr. Sterling," Frank said, "isn't the fire alarm hooked up to the electric system?"

"Yes, it is," Mr. Sterling said.

"Remember when the fire alarm went off the first day of school? You were testing it to check for any electrical problems."

"Yes, but what does that have to do with the missing dinosaur model?" Mr. Sterling said.

"Carlos was playing with the remote-control car on the same day the iguanodon disappeared," Frank said. "And you came out and told him to stop. You said you were having electrical problems in the building that day."

"Maybe the crashing noise we just heard inside wasn't the thief. Maybe it was one of the models," Frank said.

"Come to think of it," Mr. Sterling said, "I did just notice that one of the models was on the floor when I came into the auditorium to turn off the lights. Last time I saw it, I thought it was on the table. The model looked so lifelike, I was wondering if it had hopped off the table by itself."

"I think the model hopped off the table with a little help from the remote control that Carlos was using to steer his brother's car," Frank said excitedly.

"The car's wires have been getting crossed with other wires around here— like the iguanodon's," Joe said.

"That's got to be it!" Carlos said.

"Interesting idea," Mr. Sterling said. "The iguanodon was steered somewhere by accident with Carlos's remote control."

"Yes!" Frank said.

"Well!" Mr. Sterling said. His eyes were twinkling as he let Frank, Joe, and Carlos into the auditorium. "You boys know all the nooks and crannies around this place as well as I do. So let's all have a look."

"I'll check the stage area," Frank called. "Joe, you look behind the curtain."

"I'll search the costume and prop area," Mr. Sterling said.

"And I'll look around the seats and in the aisles," Carlos said. "That model has to be around here somewhere."

The group searched every inch of the auditorium. Then they sat at the edge of the stage, letting their legs dangle over the side.

Just then the door at the back of the auditorium swung open. In walked Ms. Vaughn, followed by Mark Clark and Dr. Gershwin.

"What's all this commotion?" Ms. Vaughn asked. When she saw Frank and

Joe, she said, "You boys are having a busy day. Earlier you were running in the hall, and now you're shouting in the auditorium. I wonder what will be next."

Frank could see that Ms. Vaughn had the hint of a smile on her lips.

Mr. Sterling explained everything the boys had told him.

Ms. Vaughn shook her head. "It's a very clever theory, but I'm afraid it's too late. Mr. Clark, Dr. Gershwin, and I have been in my office making the final arrangements to cancel the event."

"Can't we take one more look?" Joe pleaded. "I just know the model's here. And you said you would cancel the assembly if the model wasn't found by the *end* of the week. It's only Wednesday."

Ms. Vaughn thought for a moment as she glanced down at her clipboard.

"It might not hurt," Mr. Clark said.

"I hear they're fine detectives," Dr. Gershwin added.

"Oh, why not?" Ms. Vaughn said.

"That model just might be somewhere nearby."

"All right!" Frank said as he, Joe, and Carlos hopped off the edge of the stage.

"But keep in mind," Ms. Vaughn said, "that the model has to be in a spot where it could have been steered by the car."

"We'll look under things and around corners this time," Carlos said.

Even Ms. Vaughn joined in the search. She walked to the back of the auditorium and walked slowly to the front, checking between all the rows.

After a few minutes, Joe's voice rang out from the corner of the room, right next to the windows. "I found it!" he called.

Everyone ran to the spot where Joe was standing. There, behind a carton, was the iguanodon model. It was tangled in its plastic covering.

"It's right where Carlos's remote control steered it," Frank said.

"It was under our noses the whole time," Carlos said.

"So it was," Dr. Gershwin said.

"You boys are heroes," Mark Clark said.

The boys grinned from ear to ear. Ms. Vaughn patted each of them on the back. "I think everything should be on again tomorrow," she said. Mark Clark and Dr. Gershwin agreed.

"And we should all get to sit in the front row," Carlos said.

"I'll do even better than that," Mark Clark said, giving the boys high-fives.

The next day the boys got to school early. Mike Mendez was there waiting for them. "Carlos told me the whole story," he said.

"Are you feeling better?" Frank asked.

"Sure. And I wouldn't have missed this show for anything. Especially since you guys solved the case."

"We finally get to see the iguanodon in action. I can't wait," Joe said.

"Me, neither," Mike said.

The friends were first into the auditorium when the third and fourth grades were brought in. Frank, Joe, Chet, and Mike sat in the front row for the movie clips. During the hands-on exhibit, they got to see models from all their favorite movies.

"Look! It's the stegosaurus from *Dinos at Dawn*," Joe said. He picked up the model. Then he set it on the floor so he could make it move. "This is so neat! The remote-control device is just like the one for Mike's car," he said.

The boys touched and held several other movie models. They were able to look at how each was made, and Mark Clark answered all their questions.

After that, Dr. Gershwin talked about what paleontologists do. "We search for clues about dinosaurs."

"We search for clues, too," Joe whispered to Frank. "I guess that makes us dinosaur detectives."

The last part of the assembly was Mark Clark's special iguanodon demonstration.

Before beginning, he said, "I'm going to need a few volunteers from the audience to help me out up here."

Dozens of hands went up. Mark Clark selected Frank and Joe.

The boys helped Mr. Clark with cables and switches while he explained the model to the students and showed them how he operated it for the movie.

Before Frank and Joe returned to their seats, Mark Clark asked them to take a bow. "Without these two boys, we wouldn't be having this exhibit at all."

Frank and Joe returned to their seats while the audience cheered loudly.

At the book table, Mike bought a copy of *Making Movie Magic*. Frank and Joe bought one to share. First Dr. Gershwin autographed the inside of the books. Then

Mark Clark said, "I'd like to write something special in each of your books."

In Mike's book, he wrote: "To a future special-effects genius."

In Frank and Joe's book, he wrote: "To a great pair of detectives. Thanks for digging up the clues that solved this mystery."

"I think we should all go over to the Flavor-a-Day Ice Cream shop after school—to *dig up* some new flavors," Chet said.

"Good idea," Joe said. "Especially since we have the real *scoop* on the missing model."

"I think we should declare this case closed," Frank said with a laugh. "And we'll make no *bones* about it."

"The last time I heard that, I fell off my dinosaur laughing," Chet said as everyone filed out of the auditorium.

As the door to the auditorium slammed shut behind them, Joe said, "This has been a dino-mite case!"

BRAND-NEW SERIES!

Meet up with suspense and mystery in

FRANK AND JOE HARDY: THE CLUES BROTHERS™

#1 The Gross Ghost Mystery

Frank and Joe are making friends and meeting monsters!

#2 The Karate Clue

Somebody's kicking up a major mess!

#3 First Day, Worst Day

Everybody's mad at Joe! Is he a tattletale?

#4 Jump Shot Detectives

He shoots! He scores! He steals?

#5 Dinosaur Disaster

It's big, it's bad, it's a Bayport-asaurus! Sort-of.

By Franklin W. Dixon

Look for a brand-new story every other month
at your local bookseller

A MINSTREL® BOOK

Published by Pocket Books

1398-04